CALICO ILLUSTRATED CLASSICS

Victor Hugo's

The Hunchback of Notre Dame

ADAPTED BY: Dotti Enderle
ILLUSTRATED BY: Guy Wolek

magic Wagon

visit us at www.abdopublishing.com

Published by Magic Wagon, a division of the ABDO Group, 8000 West 78th Street, Edina, Minnesota 55439. Copyright © 2012 by Abdo Consulting Group, Inc. International copyrights reserved in all countries. All rights reserved. No part of this book may be reproduced in any form without written permission from the publisher.

Calico Chapter Books™ is a trademark and logo of Magic Wagon.

Printed in the United States of America, Melrose Park, Illinois.
052011
092011
 This book contains at least 10% recycled materials.

Original text by Victor Hugo
Adapted by Dotti Enderle
Illustrated by Guy Wolek
Edited by Stephanie Hedlund and Rochelle Baltzer
Cover and interior design by Abbey Fitzgerald

Library of Congress Cataloging-in-Publication Data

Enderle, Dotti, 1954-
  Victor Hugo's The hunchback of Notre Dame / adapted by Dotti Enderle ; illustrated by Guy Wolek.
    p. cm. -- (Calico illustrated classics)
  ISBN 978-1-61641-614-0
  1. France--History--Medieval period, 987-1515--Juvenile fiction. [1. France--History--Medieval period, 987-1515--Fiction. 2. Notre-Dame de Paris (Cathedral)--Fiction. 3. People with disabilities--Fiction. 4. Paris (France)--History--To 1515--Fiction. 5. France--History--15th century--Fiction.] I. Wolek, Guy, ill. II. Hugo, Victor, 1802-1885. Notre-Dame de Paris. III. Title.
  PZ7.E69645Vi 2011
  [Fic]--dc22
                                              2011002732

Table of Contents

Pierre Gringoire

On the morning of January 6, 1482, the church bells clanged, awakening the citizens of Paris on this joyous day. Not only was it a religious holiday known as Epiphany, but it was also the Festival of Fools, a celebration for the people.

They celebrated with fireworks, bonfires, and the planting of a May Tree. But their favorite event was electing the Pope of Fools.

People gathered early that morning outside the Palace of Justice. A mystery play would be performed at noon, and everyone wanted to sit close. The Bishop and other important guests were expected to arrive.

But the crowd grew tired of waiting and began to stir. They shouted, broke windows, and climbed the church pillars. They taunted the actors, calling them names and making fun of their clothes. Then they joined together, chanting, "The play! The play! The play!"

Pierre Gringoire, the author of the play, grew nervous. Should he start early? If he began now, the crowd would calm down, and he could avoid a riot. But what about the Bishop and other officials arriving at noon? They would be offended that he had not waited. On the other hand, there would be no play if the rowdy townspeople destroyed the stage. So Pierre made his decision. "Begin!"

The crowd whistled and cheered as the play began. Things went well for a bit, but then the officials came in one by one. Each time they were announced by name. When the Duke of Austria arrived, he brought dozens of men with him—each called individually. Every time the play had to be stopped, the crowd grew loud and unruly.

Pierre tried to keep the momentum, but it was no use. So he made a brave decision.

"Start the play again!" he announced. The actors took their places and started from the beginning.

This didn't sit well with the audience members who'd arrived early. "You idiots! We've already seen this! You can't start over!"

An official from Belgium stood. "What sort of a play is this? They're not even fighting! They barely move, and their costumes are ridiculous. I'd rather elect a Pope of Fools than be bothered with this awful performance!"

This brought a thunderous *huzzah!* from the crowd. "Pope of Fools! Let's elect the Pope of Fools!"

In the twinkling of an eye, everything was ready. A little chapel inside the majestic hall was chosen for the "Scene of Grimaces." The crowd broke the glass out of a little round

window above the door. The competitors were instructed to stand on a barrel and put their heads through the empty circle.

The chapel filled up with eager competitors, all anxious for the title of Pope of Fools. The doors were closed and the contest began.

The first face to emerge had reddish eyes, a wide gaping mouth, and a broad forehead puckered with wrinkles. A roar of laughter rose up from the spectators.

More faces popped up, one after the other. And more howls resounded from the crowd.

But then, the most hideous of all faces peeked through. The man had a mouth shaped like a horseshoe, a huge triangular nose, and jagged teeth that stuck out in every direction. A large, stubbly eyebrow sheltered his left eye, and his right eye was covered in a knotty wart.

People cheered in triumph. "Our winner! Our new Pope!" It was time to celebrate!

They stormed into the chapel to carry him, but they gasped when they saw all of him. This man had not been making a face. This was how he always looked.

His gigantic head was covered with red bristles, and between his shoulders was an enormous hump. His feet were massive and his hands monstrous. He looked like a giant who had been shattered, then put back together piece by piece.

The townspeople recognized him instantly. One cried out, "It is Quasimodo, the Cyclops! The bell ringer! The hunchback of Notre Dame!"

The students teased and taunted him. The women covered their faces. Others yelled insults.

"Look at the huge ape!"

"Oh, the ugly hunchback!"

"It's the devil himself!"

Quasimodo just stood there at the chapel door, looking gloomy and grave.

One man came up and laughed in his face. Quasimodo didn't understand that it was the

Festival of Fools. He lifted the man up and hurled him into the crowd.

The official from Belgium approached him. "You are the ugliest creature ever." He clapped his hand to the hunchback's shoulder. "You are a big fellow. I'd like to challenge you to a wrestling match."

But Quasimodo didn't stir.

"Ah!" the official cried. "The church bells have made him deaf!"

But this didn't matter to the festivalgoers. They had their Pope of Fools. They placed a robe over his back and a paper crown on his head. They hoisted him up on a litter and carried him about.

Quasimodo smiled down at all the well-shaped men and women as they left the church and paraded him down the street.

Esmeralda

Pierre Gringoire was still at the theater. He'd insisted that the play go on, even though there were so few in attendance. One by one they left, too. Only a few students remained. One pointed out the window, shouting, "It's Esmeralda! She is dancing in the square!"

The others raced to the window. They shouted, "Esmeralda!"

Pierre gave up. "It's useless."

Since night comes early in January, it was already dusk when Pierre left the hall. He was happy the day was over, yet sad that his play had failed. He desperately needed the money to pay his rent. He was already six months behind!

Pierre wandered about with nowhere to go. Everyone was still celebrating the Festival of Fools. *I might as well join them,* he told himself. He headed in the direction of the fireworks, music, and bonfires, an area called the Place de Grève.

When Pierre reached the Place he was shivering, numb, and cold. He hurried toward a magnificent bonfire that blazed in the middle

of the square. A large group of people had formed a circle around it.

"Oh, these cursed Parisians!" he cried. "They are shutting me away from the fire." But then he saw that the people were not warming themselves. They were watching a girl dancing.

Pierre watched in fascination. He was struck by her dazzling beauty. She was not tall, but her slender figure made it appear so. Her skin was tinted gold, her hair was thick and dark, and her flashing eyes danced along with her. She spun and twirled on an old Persian carpet spread out on the pavement. With her arms held high, she kept time with her tambourine.

Then the girl stopped dancing and called, "Djali!" A pretty little white goat trotted to her.

"Djali," said the girl, "it is your turn now."

She sat down and held her tambourine out. "Djali," she continued, "what month is it?"

The goat raised its leg and struck the tambourine once. The crowd applauded since it was the first month.

"Djali," said the girl, turning the tambourine the other way, "what day of the month is it?"

Djali raised his little hoof and struck the instrument six times.

The girl turned the tambourine again. "Djali, what time is it?"

Djali gave it seven blows. At that moment the town clock struck seven. The people were astounded.

"She is using witchcraft!" a bald man yelled. But his cry was drowned out by the applause.

"Djali," said the girl, "show us how the churchmen preach." The goat sat down on its rump, shaking its front hooves and bleating.

"Witchcraft!" the bald man yelled again.

The girl ignored him. She passed around her tambourine, collecting coins in all sizes. Then she came up to Pierre. She was so beautiful, staring up at him with her large, dark eyes. Sweat formed on his forehead. He wanted to give her money, but his pockets were empty.

Just then a ragged woman shouted, "Gypsy! Thief!"

The gypsy girl turned away. She began to sing, but the woman shouted at her again. "Be quiet!"

"Don't pay any attention to that beggar woman," a boy told Pierre. "She hates gypsies. She says they kidnapped her baby fifteen years ago. She clings to a tiny little baby shoe, which she claims is all she has left."

Pierre was hungry and tired. He needed to find food and shelter. But before he could get away, the Pope of Fools parade entered the Place de Grève.

The parade had grown bigger. Gypsies, beggars, and thieves had joined the procession. Their torches lit the square while they sang and chanted joyous songs.

Quasimodo still sat on the litter. He now had a look of pride on his face. He had no idea that he was a joke.

The bald man who had cursed at the gypsy pushed forward and knocked Quasimodo's wooden staff from his hand. Pierre recognized him right away.

"It's Dom Claude Frollo, the Archdeacon of Notre Dame! This one-eyed monster will tear him apart!" Pierre said.

Quasimodo leaped from the litter and in one bound was in front of Dom Frollo. The crowd gasped. But Quasimodo looked frightened and dropped to his knees.

The two made strange hand gestures to each other. Then the Archdeacon shook Quasimodo's shoulders, motioning him to rise and follow.

The crowd yelped at the priest. But Quasimodo raised his strong, clenched fists at them. He gnashed his teeth like an angry tiger.

The priest made a sign to Quasimodo, and the hunchback went forward and opened a passage for him through the crowd. Then off they went, silently, in the night.

Following a Pretty Girl

Pierre had found the gypsy girl so beautiful he decided to follow her. He watched as she and her goat turned onto a narrow street. He lingered a moment but then heard her scream.

He raced toward her. She was kicking and struggling, trying to free herself from two men who had grabbed her.

"Let me go!" she cried, twisting to break free.

"Stop!" shouted Pierre as he advanced toward her captors. But one of them turned, and he could clearly see that it was Quasimodo.

The hunchback went up and dealt him a backhanded blow. Pierre went flying back, crashing onto the pavement. Dizzy and weak, dark spots bloomed before his eyes. Within seconds he passed out.

Quasimodo then lifted the girl and draped her over his arm.

"Murder! Murder!" she screamed, pounding his massive body with her tiny fists.

But before he could get away, a horseman darted forward from a side street. It was the Captain of the King's archers.

"Let her go, you scoundrels!" He snatched the gypsy girl out of Quasimodo's arms. The hunchback stared at him in surprise.

Soon an army of archers surrounded him. They seized and bound him. He bellowed and kicked and tried to bite them. The other man who'd been with Quasimodo slipped away into the darkness.

The gypsy pulled herself onto the captain's saddle. She placed her hands on his shoulders and seemed charmed by his handsome face.

"What is your name, sir?" she asked.

"Captain Phoebus at your service," he replied.

"Thank you." She slipped off his horse and vanished into the night.

Pierre sat up, his head spinning. Then he remembered the lovely girl, her goat, and Quasimodo's massive fist. He thought about the gypsy and her captors. Yes, the hunchback was one of them, but now he remembered the other—the one who'd slipped away into the darkness. Dom Claude Frollo! But why? Why would the Archdeacon want to kidnap the girl?

While these were important questions, there was something even more important on his mind. "Egad! I am freezing!"

Pierre rose and staggered along, looking for a nice fire to warm himself. As he stumbled down the street, he came upon beggars and cripples. They held out their hands and pleaded for money. "Please, sir. Can you spare a coin?"

Pierre hung his head. He had no money. But as he was walking away, something strange happened. The beggars came charging after him. Bandages were removed. Cripples threw down their crutches. Blind men could suddenly see.

"You charlatans!" he cried.

"Yes," one beggar said, "you have entered the Court of Miracles."

Pierre looked around. He had stumbled onto a crumbled section of Paris where buildings were ramshackle and worn. All around him was decay. Here is where gypsies, thieves, and all manner of criminals gathered at night.

This is no place to be, he told himself. *I must find a way out.* But in an instant, three ragged beggars seized him.

"Take him to the king!" the beggars bellowed.

A crowd gathered. They jabbed and pushed, shoving Pierre toward a rickety old tavern. Once inside, he was led to a tattered old tramp sitting on top of a barrel.

"Our king," one beggar said, bowing. He nudged Pierre closer. "Bow to King Clopin!"

"Who are you?" King Clopin asked.

Pierre shuddered and said, "My name is Pierre Gringoire."

"And what is it you do?" the king asked. "For only thieves and beggars are allowed here."

"I am a poet," Pierre informed. "I wrote the play that was performed this morning."

"A poet?" the king shouted. "I told you only beggars and thieves are allowed."

Pierre knelt down on one knee, quaking with fear. "Then I'll become an outlaw, Your Majesty. I'll join you."

The king stroked his chin. "Hmmm. First you must pass a test."

"A test?" Pierre asked, trying not to panic.

"Yes. A test of skill," the king said.

A group of ruffians snorted and sneered as they brought out a scarecrow hanging from a noose. It wore a red coat with thousands of tiny bells.

Clopin pointed to a broken stool. "Stand on that. Get up on it!"

Pierre carefully did as he was told. The stool wobbled and shook, but it didn't topple.

"Now," Clopin said, "there is a small purse in the pocket of the dummy. You are to stand on one foot, reach in, and take out the purse."

I can manage it, Pierre thought.

The king added, "You must lift it without causing a single bell on the coat to ring."

"B-b-but," Pierre stuttered. "What if I fail? What will happen then?"

Clopin grinned, showing a mouthful of rotted teeth. "Simple. We hang you."

Pierre's heart pounded. *Stay calm. Stay calm.* He needed steady hands for this task. Slowly he raised his leg. The stool wobbled and he nearly toppled off. But he carefully tried again.

He slowly reached. His fingertips touched the pocket, but the stool shook and Pierre tumbled. He grabbed the dummy on his way down, rattling every bell on the coat.

The crowd roared with laughter.

"You failed," Clopin said. "Take him out and hang him."

"No, wait!" Pierre begged.

They placed a noose around his neck, ready to drag him away. Pierre trembled. *How do I get out of this?*

Then King Clopin held up his hand, signaling them to stop. "Of course, there may be someone here to save you. We have a special custom here. If any gypsy woman wishes to marry the prisoner, his life will be spared."

Three women came forward and looked him over.

"He has no money," said one.

"He's too thin," said another.

The third woman laughed. "I'd like to help you, but I'm already married."

"No one?" the king asked again. "Very well."

But before Clopin could order the hanging, a gypsy girl approached. "I'll marry him," she said.

Pierre recognized Esmeralda right away. He breathed a sigh of relief as the rope was removed. Someone brought out a clay jug.

"Take it," Esmeralda said, passing it over to Pierre. "You must throw it on the ground."

Pierre did what he was told. The jug crashed, breaking into four pieces.

Clopin threw up his hands. "According to gypsy law, you are now married! And because the jug broke into four pieces," the king added, "you have four years to prove to the gypsy that you are worthy."

CHAPTER 4

The Bridal Night

Pierre and Esmeralda moved to a small cozy room in the back of the tavern. Pierre watched her as she fussed over Djali.

How lucky he had been to be saved by this lovely creature. He felt like the hero in some enchanting fairy tale.

She must love me very much, he told himself. Without a word, he approached. Then he leaned toward her for a kiss.

"What are you doing?" she cried. Her dark eyes glared as she drew out a dagger. Even her goat turned, pointing his sharp horns at him.

"I don't understand," Pierre said. "If you didn't want me for your husband, then why did you save me?"

"I couldn't let you hang. Not after you'd tried to rescue me from those dreadful men."

"That's it? You're not in love with me?"

"No, I'm not," she answered. "But we can still be friends."

Pierre liked the idea. "Yes. We'll be like brother and sister."

Esmeralda smiled and put the dagger away. Then she told Djali, "You can move away from him now." Djali backed off, no longer a threat to Pierre.

Pierre couldn't help but wonder about this beautiful gypsy who had rescued him.

"What sort of man could you fall in love with?" he asked.

Her eyes sparkled. "A strong man with a helmet and a sword. One who rides with gold spurs on his heels. A man who could protect me."

Pierre blushed. Even though he had tried to save her from the hunchback, he had failed. She would never look upon him as her protector.

Then he wondered, "How did you manage to escape the hunchback?"

She shuddered. "Oh, that horrid hunchback!" She covered her face with her hands and shivered.

"Do you know why he followed you?" he asked.

"No," she replied.

They both grew silent. Esmeralda began petting Djali. But Pierre was still curious. He wanted to know everything about his lovely bride.

"Why do they call you Esmeralda?" he asked.

"I don't know for sure, but I think it's because of this." She held up a small bag that she wore around her neck. It was made of green silk. In the middle was a large piece of sparkling green glass in the shape of an emerald.

Pierre reached out for it, but she pulled the bag back. "Don't touch it. It is a very powerful charm. It could hurt you."

"Who gave it to you?" he asked.

Esmeralda didn't answer. Instead, she tucked the small bag back into her shirt.

Pierre saw how upset she was and decided to change the subject. "Were you born here in Paris?"

"No," she answered. "We came here when I was a child." Her face brightened and she asked, "But what about you? I don't even know your name."

In all the excitement of the evening, it occurred to him that he had never introduced himself. "I am Pierre Gringoire."

He went on to explain, "My parents were murdered when I was six years old and I was orphaned. I wandered the streets, begging for food. Here and there a fruitwoman would give me an apple or a baker would toss me a crust of bread. At night I hid in dark alleys.

"I came here to Paris when I was sixteen. I tried many different professions. Then I was lucky enough to meet Dom Claude Frollo, the Archdeacon of Notre Dame. He took me in and educated me. I learned mathematics and science. He even taught me Latin. But eventually, I chose to be a poet."

Esmeralda smiled. "If you are so educated, then perhaps you can answer a question for me."

"Certainly," he agreed.

"What does *Phoebus* mean?"

What? Pierre was confused. Why would she want to know that? "*Phoebus* is a Latin word. It means 'the sun.'"

"The sun!" she exclaimed, suddenly so full of happiness and wonder.

"Yes," he continued. "It was the name of an ancient god who was also an archer."

"A god!" she repeated.

At that moment, one of her bracelets accidentally fell to the ground. Pierre stooped down to pick it up, but when he lifted his head, Esmeralda was gone.

Notre Dame

Notre Dame is a magnificent church with intricate carvings and massive bell towers. Being a place of worship, it was not uncommon for infants to be left there in hopes someone would adopt them. Sixteen years before the Festival of Fools, a baby had been abandoned on the church steps.

Several women hovered over the infant, cringing at the sight.

"What is it?" one asked.

"I don't know," answered another, "but it must be a sin just to look at it."

"I don't think it's a child. It's far too ugly!" said another. "It's a misshapen ape."

Indeed, the poor child's head was deformed. It had a forest of red hair, one closed eye, and another that wept. In its mouth were several crooked teeth that seemed to be searching for something to chew.

None of the women dared touch him.

"What's to become of it?" one of them asked. "No woman would ever want to nurse it."

Another added, "It should not be allowed to live."

Dom Claude Frollo, a young priest at the time, heard the women's cries. "What have we here?" he asked, looking at the squirming infant.

The women pointed to the child. "It is an abomination," one told him.

"Be that as it may," he said, "I shall adopt him." Dom Claude picked up the child and found that it did indeed look like a monster. The poor thing had a wart covering his left eye. His head was so close to his shoulders it looked like he had no neck. And his back was arched with a hump.

This didn't matter to Dom Claude. He baptized the baby. Because the child was found on Quasimodo Sunday, he named him Quasimodo.

The child grew up in Notre Dame and was given the job of the bell ringer.

Because of his deformity, Quasimodo was cut off from society and not allowed outside. Since he spent all his time within the church, he'd grown attached to the huge cathedral. There was not one crevice of the cathedral that he had not explored.

From the hidden depths to the towering roof, he knew every inch. He'd climb the outside by swinging from one sculpture to another. And yet he never got frightened or dizzy.

Because of Quasimodo's deformities, Claude Frollo had a difficult time teaching him to speak. And to make matters worse, the clanging of the church bells had made the poor hunchback deaf. The Archdeacon could only

communicate with him through various signs and gestures.

Quasimodo rang the bells by climbing and swinging from the ropes. He took pride in his job, thinking of the bells as his friends. His only human friend was Claude Frollo. The hunchback was always faithful to him and would do anything his master asked—even if the task was a nasty crime!

The day after the Festival of Fools, Quasimodo was taken into court for attempting to kidnap the gypsy. His arms were bound behind his back.

It seemed the town judge was having a bad day. The festival was a busy time for pickpockets and vandals, and many had already been through his courtroom. His patience was wearing thin. So when Quasimodo appeared before him, the judge was anxious to move along.

"What is your name?" the judge asked.

Since Quasimodo was deaf, he had no way of knowing what was said. He stood still, staring.

The judge continued. "What is your job?"

Still Quasimodo was silent. The people in the courtroom began to whisper, glancing at each other.

"That will do," the judge said. Then he spoke harshly to Quasimodo. "You are accused of attempting to kidnap a woman and resisting arrest. What do you have to say for yourself?"

Because the judge didn't know that Quasimodo was deaf, his question caused the spectators in the courtroom to burst out laughing. Quasimodo thought it was a joke. He turned toward them and shrugged his hump.

"How dare you insult me!" the judge raged. He pointed a finger at Quasimodo. "Are you aware of your crimes?"

The hunchback tried hard to understand, but he thought the judge was asking his name. "Quasimodo," he answered.

This brought more laughter throughout the courtroom. The judge flushed with fury. "How dare you make fun of me!"

Quasimodo thought he was being asked his occupation. "Bell ringer of Notre Dame," he said.

The judge lost all patience. "You wretch!" Then he pronounced Quasimodo's sentence. "Take this fellow to the pillory at the Place de Grève. Let him be bound, flogged, and turned for one hour."

They tied Quasimodo to a cart and brought him to a raised platform where all the spectators could see. It was the same spot where he had been crowned the Pope of Fools.

Quasimodo was bound with cords and placed on his knees upon the wheel of the pillory. They ripped off his shirt so that he could feel every agonizing bite of the whip. The same spectators who had cheered for him as their pope, now shouted, spit, and threw things at him.

Quasimodo stayed perfectly still. But the wheel began to turn, and the first lash of the whip came down hard on his back. He tugged and twisted with pain.

Then came the second lash, then the third. Then another and another. Blood trickled in a hundred little streams down his shoulders. He moaned, then finally gave into the pain. Closing his eye, he sadly dropped his head.

CHAPTER 6

A Tear for a Drop of Water

When the beating ended, Quasimodo was turned round and round for another hour. The crowd continued to scream and hurl things.

But then Quasimodo saw a glimmer of hope. Dom Claude Frollo, his only friend, rode up on his horse. Quasimodo was relieved to see the Archdeacon. He knew he'd been saved.

But Dom Claude made no attempt to help him. Without a word, he gently rode away.

Quasimodo couldn't believe it. Claude Frollo had always been a father to him. How could he turn his back now when he needed him most? Again he hung his head, tears trickling. He didn't know what was worse, the pain he endured from the whip, or the pain of abandonment.

Quasimodo's throat was so raw and dry he could barely swallow. Suddenly angry, he struggled in his chains, rattling the wheel. He cried out in a hoarse and furious voice. "Water!"

The crowd laughed and pointed, adding to his anger. His face turned purple and glistened with sweat. His eye glared wildly. His mouth foamed with rage and agony, and his tongue lolled to the side. He looked about the crowd anxiously. "Water!"

This brought even more laughter. They threw stones and called him names.

"Water!" he roared for the third time. He knelt on the pillory, panting like a thirsty pup.

But then the crowd parted. A young woman approached. She was followed by a little white goat. In her hand she held a tambourine.

Quasimodo's eye sparkled. It was the gypsy he had tried to carry off the night before. She was why he was being punished. Was she coming for revenge?

Quasimodo watched Esmeralda as she gently came up the steps. Without uttering a word, she approached him. He jerked back, trying to avoid her, but she pulled a flask of water from her belt and gently lifted it to his lips.

A tear fell from his bloodshot eye and trickled down his deformed face.

The crowd was also moved by her gesture. They clapped their hands, shouting, "Huzza! Huzza!"

It was at that moment that an old woman, peering from a barred window, shouted, "A curse upon you, gypsy girl! You are cursed! Cursed! Cursed! You will be the one on that pillory one day!"

Esmeralda turned pale as she rushed down the steps. But the old recluse still taunted her. "Get away, you gypsy child-stealer! You are cursed!"

By now Quasimodo's punishment had ended. He was set free and the mob dispersed.

The Danger of Confiding Secrets to a Goat

Several weeks later, on a beautiful spring day in Paris, Dame Aloise and her daughter, Fleur-de-lys de Gondelaurier, were sitting in her apartment just across from Notre Dame. Several of Fleur-de-lys's friends were there, chatting and tittering.

Captain Phoebus sat among them. He was engaged to Fleur-de-lys, but it was an arranged marriage. He was bored by it all and daydreamed of being somewhere else.

Dame Aloise loved bragging about her daughter. She tugged on the captain's sleeve, worried that he had lost interest.

"Look at my daughter," she whispered. "You are so lucky to have her as your fiancée. She has the elegance of a swan."

"Yes, indeed," he said, his mind wandering the whole time.

"Go on and talk to her," she said, pushing him toward Fleur-de-lys. "You seem so shy."

To please Dame Aloise, the captain approached his future bride. Phoebus stared, not knowing what to say. He should tell her how lovely she was, and how he couldn't wait till they were married. But he didn't feel any of those things.

One of Fleur-de-lys's guests happened to glance out the window. "Come look! Look at that pretty girl down there dancing and playing the tambourine."

Fleur-de-lys turned to Phoebus. "Isn't that the girl you rescued several weeks ago?"

The captain looked down at the dancing gypsy. "I believe it is." She was so beautiful that more and more he hated the idea of getting married. "Yes, that is her goat."

Then Fleur-de-lys pointed across the square. "Who is that man? The one dressed in black?"

They all looked up. A man was standing on a balcony of the North Tower. He was as still as a statue, staring down at the street below.

"Oh! It is the Archdeacon," Fleur-de-lys said.

Phoebus squinted toward the tower. "You must have good sight to recognize him at that distance!"

"But look at how he watches the dancing girl," one of the women exclaimed.

"She should beware," Fleur-de-lys said. "The Archdeacon does not like gypsies."

"That's a shame," said another of her guests. "She dances beautifully."

Fleur-de-lys's eyes flashed. "Since you know her, Phoebus, why don't you ask her to come dance for us? We would love it."

"Yes, please!" the others cried, bouncing with excitement.

"I'm sure she has forgotten me," Phoebus said. "And I don't even know her name."

"Please! Please!" they all begged.

Phoebus surrendered. "I will try."

He leaned out the window and shouted, "Young woman!"

The dancer paused for a moment before looking up in his direction. Her eyes sparkled when she saw him, and she stood motionless.

"Dancer!" he called down to her.

She still stared up at him, blushing deeply as though every drop of blood had rushed to her cheeks. Then she tucked her tambourine under her arm and made her way through the circle of spectators. With slow, careful steps, she walked toward the home where she had been called.

Moments later, the door was opened and Esmeralda stepped in, out of breath, flushed, and flurried.

The mood in the room suddenly changed. All the young women in Fleur-de-lys's apartment were quite lovely, and they each wanted to capture the attention of the handsome officer who stood among them.

But when they saw Esmeralda, their smiles turned to scowls. Her beauty overshadowed everything. The young ladies were dazzled and filled with envy.

The captain finally broke the silence. "What a charming creature you are!"

It seemed Dame Aloise was the only one who didn't feel jealous. "Come here, my girl."

Esmeralda took a few steps forward. Phoebus was so taken with this girl's radiance that he hurried over to her.

"I don't know if you remember me or not—"

"Oh yes!" she said, interrupting him with a smile and a look of kindness.

Hmmm . . . she has a very good memory, Fleur-de-lys observed.

"Why was it," Phoebus asked, "that you slipped away in such a hurry the other night? Did I frighten you?"

"Of course not," she answered.

Phoebus could barely take his eyes off her. "We captured the one-eyed hunchback who tried to abduct you. You'll not have to worry about him again. He's been punished."

"Yes," she said, thinking of the sad scene at the pillory. "Poor fellow."

She actually felt sorry for him? Phoebus was astounded. "Don't pity him. He's a rotten, worthless ogre. He got what he deserved."

Fleur-de-lys could see that the captain was enchanted by the gypsy and turned green with envy. "Naturally she would pity that horrid beast. Look at her. She's no better. What decent woman would wear those dreadful clothes?"

"Yes," one of the ladies agreed. "How can you run about on the streets with such a short skirt and no veil?"

"My dear," Fleur-de-lys sneered, "you should be arrested just for wearing that belt!"

All of the ladies nodded. Since they couldn't say anything bad about Esmeralda's beauty, they made fun of her clothes.

"Look at you," another chimed in. "If you would cover your arms with decent sleeves, they wouldn't be sunburned."

They continued to laugh and jeer as though Esmeralda was not even there. Their remarks stung, making her furious. But she kept her feelings to herself, afraid they'd ask her to leave. She stood quiet and still, gazing up at Phoebus with a troubled and gentle look.

He felt sorry for her. "Don't listen to them," he said. "I like the way you're dressed. It adds to your beauty."

Suddenly Dame Aloise cried out, "Dear me! What is that nasty beast beside her?"

Esmeralda got down on her knees and pressed her head against her pet goat.

"Wait," one of the ladies said, "I have heard that she is a witch and that her goat does amazing tricks."

"I want to see it," said another. "Have your goat perform for us."

"I don't know what you mean," Esmeralda quietly replied. She had to be extra careful. They already hated her.

"Show us some magic or witchcraft," the lady said.

Esmeralda continued petting Djali without a word. Fleur-de-lys moved closer and pointed to a small bag hanging around the goat's neck. "What is that?"

Esmeralda raised her large eyes toward her. "It is a secret meant only for me."

Fleur-de-lys stomped her foot. "I want to know what your secret is."

Esmeralda pulled the goat closer.

Dame Aloise turned up her nose. "Girl," she said sharply, "if you or your goat are not going to dance, then you should leave this instant."

Esmeralda did not reply. She simply rose and walked to the door. Then she turned toward Phoebus, her eyes glistening with tears.

"Please don't go," he pleaded. "Come back and dance for us. We don't even know your name."

"It's Esmeralda," she said, her eyes fixed upon him.

The young ladies burst out laughing.

"What a dreadful name!" one cried out. "With a name like that, she must be a witch."

While they continued to taunt her, someone opened the small bag that hung around Djali's neck. Out tumbled several small wooden tiles, each containing a letter of the alphabet.

As soon as they spilled onto the floor, the goat lifted his hoof and shuffled them. Then, one by one, he lined them up to spell a word.

Fleur-de-lys shuddered. "Oh my!"

Djali had arranged the tiles to form the name Phoebus.

"This was a secret," Esmeralda cried as she bent down to scoop them up. She began to tremble and tears slid down her cheeks.

"You see!" Fleur-de-lys thundered as she pointed to the gypsy. "It's true. She is a witch!"

Dame Aloise rushed forward. "Out!" she yelled. "Take your goat and get out of here at once!"

Esmeralda and Djali hurried out the door.

Captain Phoebus wavered a moment, not sure what to do. He looked at the rude women briefly, then turned and followed the gypsy girl.

The Priest

The Archdeacon, Claude Frollo, stood atop the North Tower, watching the gypsy girl. She danced and twirled, spinning the tambourine on the tip of her finger. But he also noticed a man in a red and yellow coat next to her, balancing a chair between his teeth.

"Who is that man?" he muttered, clearly upset. "The gypsy always dances alone. Where did he come from?"

Dom Claude vaulted down the spiral staircase and out onto the street. By the time he reached the square, the gypsy had gone. He rushed up to the man in the red and yellow coat.

"Where did she go?" he asked.

The man turned around and the Archdeacon recognized him immediately. "You're Pierre Gringoire, the poet. What are you doing out here?"

Dom Claude's shouts startled Pierre. He flinched, losing his balance. The chair came crashing down to the pavement.

"This makes no sense," Dom Claude went on. "You're a street performer?"

Pierre hung his head. "I am ashamed to admit it. I am a complete failure as a poet. But I must eat. Doing these balancing tricks brings enough money to buy bread."

Desperate for answers, the Archdeacon said, "I saw you performing alongside the gypsy. She always works alone. Why would she allow it?"

Pierre stood tall. "Because we are married."

"What!" Dom Claude's eyes glared like fire. "Have you stooped so low that you would marry a gypsy?!" Secretly, he was wickedly jealous.

"It's not a real marriage," Pierre assured him. "We're more like brother and sister." He told

Dom Claude how Esmeralda had rescued him and about breaking the jug.

"Gypsies are superstitious people," Pierre continued. "Especially Esmeralda."

"What do you mean?" the Archdeacon asked, intrigued.

Pierre picked up the toppled chair and leaned against it. "My wife wears a charm around her neck. She believes that one day it will help her find her true parents."

The Archdeacon crossed his arms. "Do you believe such nonsense?" he scoffed.

Pierre shrugged. "It's the way of the gypsies. I don't question it. They are all very, very close. And they love Esmeralda dearly. They look after her. There are only two people that she's truly afraid of—the old recluse who shouts at her from the barred window and a priest who continually stares down at her. She's never met him, but he scares her."

The Archdeacon knew that she was afraid of him, but he would eventually change that.

Pierre continued, "I can see why everyone loves her so much. She's sweet and kind, and she loves that clever little goat. I'm amazed at all the things it can do. It only took her two months to teach it how to spell the word *Phoebus* with some wooden tiles."

Dom Claude asked, "Why Phoebus?"

"I don't know," Pierre replied. "Maybe she thinks the word has some type of secret magic."

"Are you sure," Dom Claude asked with a piercing look, "that it is only a word and not a name?"

The poet thought for a moment. "Whose name could it be?"

Dom Claude suddenly felt trapped. "How should I know?"

Pierre scratched his chin, then asked Claude, "Why are you asking me all these questions?"

The Archdeacon squirmed, turning a crimson shade of red. "I-I-I am only interested in your welfare," he said. Embarrassed, he quickly turned and rushed back to the cathedral.

The Two Men in Black

Later that day, Dom Claude was strolling along the square when he passed by two men laughing and chatting.

"What is the matter, Phoebus?" one man said.

The Archdeacon froze. *Phoebus? Could this be the person that Pierre had mentioned earlier?* He quickly moved into the shadows to listen.

"Blood and thunder!" Phoebus cursed. "Those wretched women! They are so cruel."

"Calm down," his companion said. "Go with me to the tavern. That'll take your mind off of it and you can relax."

Phoebus nodded. "That's an excellent idea."

Dom Claude had to know more about this man. He wrapped his cloak around himself and followed, making sure they didn't see him slinking behind. But he was close enough to hear what they were saying.

As they turned the corner, Phoebus pulled back. "Wait!" he said to his friend. "The gypsy girl. I can hear her tambourine. She's just up the street. I can't let her see me."

Intrigued, Dom Claude drew in closer. He didn't want to miss a word.

"Do you know her?" the man asked Phoebus.

The Captain grinned. "Indeed. I have charmed her. She has agreed to meet me tonight at seven o'clock."

"Do you think she'll come?"

Phoebus threw his head back and laughed. "Of course she will!"

The man clapped Phoebus on the back. "Captain, you are one lucky fellow."

The Archdeacon heard every syllable of the conversation. He gritted his teeth and seethed with anger. He had to follow them and see if the gypsy really would come to meet the captain.

The two men headed into the busy tavern and Dom Frollo waited. He stayed hidden and watched the clock on the tower, knowing that they would be out before seven o'clock.

Finally, at a quarter till seven both men came stumbling out. They were grinning and singing as they swayed with their arms around each other.

"Well now," Phoebus said, "I must be on my way. I can't keep my little gypsy girl waiting."

The two men shook hands and parted.

Phoebus walked along, glancing over his shoulder now and again. He had an odd feeling that someone was behind him. Finally he turned and spoke to the phantom follower. "If you are a robber then you're out of luck. I don't have any money."

The man in the dark cloak reached out and grasped the captain's arm. He kept his head down to hide his face.

"Captain Phoebus," he said.

Phoebus tried to pull his arm away, but the man held tight. "You know my name?" Phoebus asked the stranger.

The man in the cloak looked up, his eyes dark and piercing. "Not only do I know your name, but I also know where you are going."

"What is it you want?" the captain asked.

"I simply want to know her name," the stranger replied.

The captain hesitated, then said, "Esmeralda."

"You liar!" the cloaked man raged.

Phoebus jerked his arm free of the stranger's grasp. "You dare call me a liar? Draw your sword immediately!" Phoebus pulled his own sword from its scabbard and held it up.

But the man in the cloak stepped away. "It's nearly seven. If you take the time to fight me, you'll miss your appointment with the gypsy."

The captain sheathed his glistening sword. "You are right. I have no time for you."

He turned to go, but the man said, "If you're meeting her at a tavern, you'll need money. Here." He drew out a small money bag and held it up.

"That's generous," Phoebus said, reaching for it.

But the stranger pulled it back. "I'll give it to you on one condition. Let me follow you. I want to see for myself that you are really meeting Esmeralda. I promise she won't see me."

The captain said, "It doesn't matter to me. If you want to come along then let's go." He took the money and they hurried away.

The Dagger

Captain Phoebus and Dom Claude soon arrived at the tavern where Esmeralda had agreed to meet. The place was dim and dirty, and people sat with their heads hanging.

The two men pushed through and went straight to the back. They met with a toothless old woman in rags. Deep wrinkles creased her face and gray whiskers sprouted from her chin.

"Follow me," she said, leading them up the stairs.

They were taken into a small, dusty room. Cobwebs stretched in every corner. The only furniture was two rickety stools and a wobbly table.

When the old woman left, Phoebus pointed to a small closet. "Over there." Dom Claude stepped in it and closed the door. It was the perfect hiding place.

"I shall go out and wait for Esmeralda," Phoebus said.

Dom Claude felt around in the tight, dark space. It was narrow and cramped. He waited a full fifteen minutes before hearing a creaking on the staircase. Someone was coming up. He peeked through a crevice in the wall.

The door opened and Phoebus came in along with the gypsy and her goat. Dom Claude's heart nearly stopped. She was so beautiful! He couldn't take his eyes off of her.

She shivered and pulled her shawl tightly around her neck. "I shouldn't be here," she said.

"Don't be silly," Phoebus replied. "Why shouldn't you be here?"

Esmeralda strolled across the room. "People already think wicked things about me. What if they knew I was all alone with you?"

Phoebus smiled. "Never mind what people think. How can it be wrong if you love me?"

Esmeralda relaxed. "Oh yes. I do love you!" She rushed to him and he put his arms around her.

"Oh, Esmeralda! How lucky I am," Phoebus said. "Please tell me, why do you love me?"

Her eyes sparkled as she gazed up at him. "I love you because you are kind and handsome. And you saved my life. I could never repay you for that."

Dom Claude clutched his hands into fists, wanting to pound the door. He raged with jealousy.

Then Esmeralda asked the captain, "Do you love me?"

"With all my life," Phoebus answered. Then he swept her into a kiss.

He doesn't deserve her! Dom Claude thought.

Esmeralda swooned. "Then we should get married."

Phoebus took a step back, his eyes wide. "What? Why should we get married?"

She turned sickly pale and hung her head.

Dom Claude quivered and boiled as he watched this from the dark closet. It was clear that Phoebus didn't really love the gypsy girl. He was only taking advantage of her. He was there to steal kisses.

Phoebus drew her close again, noticing a little bag that hung around her neck. "What is this?" he said, lifting it up.

"Do not touch it!" she cried, drawing her shawl tight again. "It is a special charm. It is how my family will find me . . . as long as I do nothing wrong."

She suddenly seemed distressed. "I must go. Being here is wrong. If I stay, my real parents will never find me."

"I see," Phoebus said, sounding sneaky, "so you don't really love me."

"Yes, I do, but—"

Before she could finish the sentence, Phoebus kissed her again. But at that moment a dark shadow fell over them. When Esmeralda looked up, she saw the twisted, scowling face of a man with a dagger. And in an instant, he plunged the knife into the captain's back. Phoebus shrieked in pain, staggered, then fell to the floor.

Esmeralda stumbled back, too terrified to scream. The intruder paused, staring into her eyes. Then fear overtook her and she fainted on the spot.

When Esmeralda awoke, there were soldiers pacing about the room. Then she remembered the man who'd stormed out of the closet and attacked Phoebus. She'd seen him before. He was the one who stood on the North Tower watching her dance.

As she sat up, she saw two men carrying Phoebus out of the room. His arms were limp and blood dripped from his coat. Tears streamed from her eyes. Was he dead? She couldn't tell.

It was then that one of the soldiers grabbed her arm and jerked her up off the floor. "She's the one," he cried. "This no good gypsy witch killed Captain Phoebus!"

"Wait! No! No! It wasn't me!" she pleaded.

"Come along!" The soldier jerked her toward the door, while another grabbed Djali. They shoved them into a cart and took them off to jail.

CHAPTER 11

The Mysterious Monk

Back in the Court of Miracles everyone was wondering about Esmeralda. It had been more than a month since they'd seen her or Djali. Pierre Gringoire was especially worried. When he asked around, someone told him they'd seen the gypsy walking with an officer. But that was weeks ago.

Pierre's life had gone on as usual. He had continued to entertain in the streets without his wife by his side. Then one day as he passed by the prison, he heard a lively commotion.

"What's going on?" Pierre ask a young man standing by the steps.

"I don't know for sure," the man said, "but I am told that a woman is on trial for murdering an officer. They say she's a witch."

Pierre was far too curious to walk away. Instead, he pushed in with the crowd and took a seat in the back. He saw the prisoner, shackled in chains, but she was turned away from him. He couldn't see her face.

Soon the trial was underway. A withered old woman took the stand.

"I can tell you exactly what happened," the old woman testified. "Two men came in that night and asked for a room. One was the captain. The other man had a black cloak drawn around him so I didn't see his face. Then later, the girl came in and joined them upstairs.

"I just went about my business, but then I heard this horrible cry. I looked outside and that's when I saw something black drop down from the window above. It looked just like a ghost dressed up as a priest."

Everyone in the courtroom gasped.

"Several of us rushed up there," the old woman went on. "That's when we saw the captain lying on the floor, covered in blood.

A large silver dagger was buried in his back."
Then the old woman pointed at the prisoner.
"And she was there. I think this gypsy conjured
a spell to have the officer killed!"

There was shuffling and muttering
throughout the courtroom.

Witchcraft? Pierre thought.

"Did you do it?" the judge asked the gypsy.
"Did you murder Captain Phoebus?"

"No!" she cried. "No!" That's when she
turned pleadingly toward the crowd.

Pierre's heart froze. It was Esmeralda! It
was his wife! Her skin was so pale and her eyes
were dark and hollow.

"Where is Phoebus?" Esmeralda demanded.
"I've been told that he is dead, but I want to see
for myself!"

"Silence!" the judge shouted.

"Please, I have to know," she begged. "If
Captain Phoebus is alive, you must tell me."

"That is enough!" the judge thundered.
"Now, bring in the other prisoner."

All eyes grew wide when the guard led a small white goat into the courtroom.

Pierre broke into a sweat. Djali? Surely they don't think that Djali is capable of sorcery.

"Stop!" he cried. "He is just an innocent goat."

"Silence!" the judge demanded. Then he turned to the guard. "Can you prove that this goat is a witch?"

The guard held out Esmeralda's tambourine, then said, "Observe." Djali performed his usual tricks, counting out the day, month, and year on the jangling instrument. Next the guard emptied the small pouch of letters onto the floor. Djali sorted them out, spelling the word *Phoebus*.

The spectators watched, wide-eyed and horror-stricken. "The devil!" one shouted. "This goat is surely the devil!"

Esmeralda sat quietly, her eyes downcast. She looked helpless and alone.

The judge turned to her and jeered. "Girl, you and your goat have used sorcery to bewitch and murder Captain Phoebus. Do you deny this?"

"Of course," she answered. "I could never hurt my dear Phoebus."

The judge curled his lip angrily. "Why do you persist in denying it?"

Her eyes flashed as she rose from her seat. "Because I am innocent," she said in a fearful tone.

The judge grew impatient. "Then how do you explain it? You and your goat were the only ones there."

"I don't know," she said. "I already told you. There was a priest—a stranger. He watches me and follows me."

The judge sighed. He turned to the guard. "Since the prisoner refuses to admit her guilt, you shall take her to the dungeon to be tortured."

"No, wait!" Esmeralda cried, quivering all over. But the guard grabbed her arm and jerked her out of the courtroom.

Leave All Hope Behind

Esmeralda was taken down into a musky, dark dungeon with no windows or light. The only way in or out was through a strong iron door with multiple locks. A large furnace stood near the wall with a blazing fire that threw off a red glare. There were tools of torture scattered about in the ashes. The poor girl was struck with horror when she saw them. Would they be using them on her?

"One last time," the guard said, "do you deny murdering the captain?"

"Yes," she replied softly. "I did not do it. You must believe me."

But the guard just shook his head. "If you won't confess, then we must apply the boot."

He lifted her bare foot and placed it inside a heavy iron shoe.

"No! No! No!" she pleaded. But the guard continued his task. He tightened a screw on the boot that caused it to squeeze against her foot. The pain was horrendous, and her screams echoed through the chamber.

"Do you still deny it?" the guard asked.

"I didn't do it!"

He tightened the screw some more. Esmeralda nearly fainted from the pain. "Please, have mercy!"

"Confess, woman!" the guard yelled. "Admit you're a witch! You killed the captain. Admit it!" He tightened the screw again and she thought the bones in her foot might shatter into small splinters.

"Yes! Yes! I confess! Please stop!"

He sneered as he slowly loosened the screw.

Esmeralda wilted against him, her spirit broken.

"At last," the guard said, pulling her throbbing foot from the boot. "The judge will deal with you now."

He led her back to the courtroom.

The judge looked down on her with dark eyes. "Gypsy girl, you have confessed to the murder of Captain Phoebus. You shall remain in prison until a day chosen by the King. You will then be taken to the Place de Grève where you and your goat will both be hanged."

Esmeralda lowered her head and wept. "This must be a dream!"

Then rough, heavy hands carried her away.

Esmeralda was thrust into a damp jail cell with no heat or lamp. Her foot was swollen from the torture boot, and it hurt even more from the heavy chain they'd clamped around her ankle.

Once a day the guard would bring her a piece of bread and a cup of water. His entrance and exit were the only times she saw any light.

She slept on a bed of scratchy straw, and she thought frequently of the events that led her here—her wonderful Phoebus, the dark priest, the dagger, the murder. How could this nightmare be happening to her?

Several days had passed when the door to her cell opened and someone slipped in. A dark, robed figure descended the steps. She tried to see his face, but it was concealed by a large hood.

"Who is there?" she asked, squinting to see her visitor.

"Just a priest," he answered.

There was something about him that made her shudder. The priest drew closer. "Are you prepared?"

She wasn't sure what he meant.

"Are you prepared to die?" he asked.

Confusion and fear filled her. "How soon?"

He paused a moment, then said, "Tomorrow."

Her head sank.

"Oh, sweet gypsy, you must be so unhappy," the priest said.

Her teeth chattered as she rubbed her hands together. "I am so very cold."

He held up the lantern and looked around the dungeon. "This is horrendous! No light? No fire? Not even a pitcher of water."

She burst into tears. "I hate it! I want to leave here!"

"Then come with me," he said, clutching her arm. His touch felt like the icy hand of death.

"Who are you?" she asked.

He pushed back his hood revealing his sinister face. Oh no! The man with the dagger! The very man who had caused her world to collapse.

"It is you!" She tried to break free, but he held her arm tight.

His eyes softened. "Are you afraid of me?" he asked.

"Yes!" she cried, struggling against his grasp. "You are the one who killed my Phoebus!

You are the reason they hurled me into this dungeon. Why have you done this? Do you hate me so much that you would ruin my life?"

"I don't hate you," he said. "I love you!"

She tried pulling away again, but he said, "Listen to me. I was a proud priest, one who everybody looked up to. And as a man of God, I never even thought of women. Then I saw you dancing on the square. You were so lovely, and you moved so beautifully. But when I saw your little goat with you, I knew you had bewitched me. Only witches associate with goats. You had me spellbound. I wanted you for myself. I tried to carry you off, but that pesky officer came and rescued you."

"Oh, my Phoebus," she uttered.

"Don't even speak his name! He has ruined us both! He did not love you. He was merely playing with your heart. I am the one who loves you, Esmeralda. Please have pity on me."

He fell to his knees on the cold stone floor. "I beg you, do not turn away from me. I love you.

Please go with me. I could help you escape. We could run away together."

She laughed in his face. "I would never run off with you. I don't consort with murderers. Your hands are still bloody from your dagger."

"Esmeralda, listen to me," he said. "You will die tomorrow. Let me save you!"

She seized his arm and fixed her eyes intently on him. "What about my Phoebus? Have you seen him?"

"He is dead," he answered, loosening his arm from her grasp.

She rushed upon him like an enraged tigress. "Then I don't want to live," she said coldly. "Get out, you monster! I will never go with you!"

The priest stumbled up the steps and pushed through the door.

Esmeralda fell onto her bed of straw and sobbed.

CHAPTER
13

The Mother

It was one of those mornings in May when the sky was a rich, deep blue. The old recluse sat by her barred window listening to the rumbling of wheels, the tramp of horses, and the clanking of iron in the Place de Grève. In her lap she held a tiny shoe.

"Oh my child! My child!" she wailed. She had kept this shoe for fifteen years. It was all that was left of her sweet baby daughter who had been stolen by gypsies.

Her grief was quickly interrupted by the sound of voices just beneath her window. Two boys were chattering about the crowd gathering in the square.

"They are going to hang the gypsy today," one boy said to the other.

The old woman rushed to her window and peered out. A gallows had been built with a heavy hangman's noose dangling from it. A priest stood close by. She recognized him immediately. It was Dom Claude.

"Father," she called to him, "is it true they are hanging a gypsy?"

"That should make you happy," he gruffed. "You hate gypsies with all your heart."

"Can you blame me? They are child-stealers! They took my little girl and left me brokenhearted. But there is one that I truly hate above all others. She's a dancing girl, about the same age my daughter would've been if those filthy gypsies hadn't murdered her. My daughter is dead, yet they allow this witch to live. My blood boils just thinking about it!"

"Well, you can rejoice today," the Archdeacon said, cold as a statue. "She is the very one they intend to hang."

"Thank goodness!" she cried.

As it turned out, Phoebus was alive. He had only been wounded by the Archdeacon's dagger and slipped away before they could pronounce him dead. He had heard about the trial while commanding his troops outside of Paris, but he wanted no part of it.

Why should I bother with her? he told himself. *She probably is a witch.*

If he appeared now it would hurt his relationship with Fleur-de-lys. He couldn't risk that. Not only was she beautiful, but she was also extremely wealthy.

Two months had already passed when he went to see her in Paris. She broke into tears when he told her he'd been wounded. "It was nothing. Just a battle wound that easily healed."

The two of them stood on the balcony, watching the commotion below. A mob booed and jeered as a cart entered, carrying the trembling gypsy girl.

"Oh, look," Fleur-de-lys said to Phoebus. "There is the gypsy and her goat."

Phoebus froze. "W-w-what gypsy with a goat?" he stammered.

"Don't you remember? She is the one whose goat could spell your name."

He stayed quiet and still, watching the activities in the square.

Poor Esmeralda never raised her eyes. Tears glistened on her cheeks. A hush fell over the crowd as two guards escorted her from the cart and led her up the steps of the cathedral. Overcome with terror, her white lips silently repeated one word over and over. "Phoebus. Phoebus. Phoebus."

A procession of priests emerged from the church. She fixed her gaze on one in particular. "Oh!" she muttered to herself. "There he is again. The priest!"

It was the Archdeacon, Dom Claude Frollo. His face was like a death mask, as pale as marble. He slunk close and placed a yellow candle in her hand.

"Gypsy, have you prayed to God for forgiveness?" Then lowering his voice he said, "It is not too late. I can still save you."

Esmeralda tried to push back. "Get away from me, or I'll tell the authorities that you are the one who attacked my Phoebus."

A ghastly grin crossed his face. "They will never believe you."

She gazed into his dark eyes. "What have you done with my Phoebus?"

"He is dead," Dom Claude said.

At that moment, he looked upward and saw the captain standing with Fleur-de-lys. He shuddered at the sight. But then his face twisted into a violent sneer.

"Well then, die!" he whispered to Esmeralda. He lowered his head and rejoined the train of priests.

The condemned girl stood motionless, waiting to be hanged. How had this happened to her? She wanted to claw the evil priest. But then she raised her eyes above the crowd. Spectators watched from windows and roofs. Then she spotted him. Phoebus! He was alive!

"Phoebus!" she cried. "My Phoebus!" She would have stretched her arms out had they not been tied behind her back.

He uttered something to Fleur-de-lys, and they withdrew back into the apartment.

Something flashed through her mind. *Oh no! He thinks it was me. He thinks I'm the one who tried to kill him. That's why he turned away.* Overcome with grief, her world went black, and she collapsed to the pavement.

The hangman moved forward. "Let's get on with it!"

The priests, the crowd, and the guards were so busy watching Esmeralda that they didn't notice the stranger leaning over a railing of Notre Dame. If it had not been for his red and purple clothes, he could have been mistaken for one of the stone gargoyles that perched on the cathedral.

With lightning speed, he seized a rope, swung downward, and knocked away two of

the guards. Then, sweeping the girl into his arms, he rushed back to the cathedral, holding her above his head.

"Sanctuary!" he shouted. "Sanctuary!"

Quasimodo's eyes sparkled with joy as the crowd repeated his chant. "Sanctuary! Sanctuary!"

The guards glanced at each other, not sure what to do. The cathedral was a holy place of protection. They were not allowed to go in and arrest someone or to bring a prisoner out. Esmeralda was safe there.

The crowd cheered Quasimodo, and at that moment, he felt like a hero. The same people who had made him an outcast now looked on him with approval.

He hurried into the church, made his way up, then appeared on the gallery. Again he held her up, shouting, "Sanctuary! Sanctuary!"

He disappeared again, then made a third appearance atop the great bell tower. He raised her high above his head to proudly show the city that he had saved her. And with a thundering voice, he cried out to all, "Sanctuary! Sanctuary! Sanctuary!"

CHAPTER
14
Deaf

Esmeralda awoke to the sounds of the city far below. When she opened her eyes, the bell ringer sat hovering about her.

"Why did you save me?" she asked him.

He looked at her like he was trying to understand. But because of his deafness, he couldn't make out a single word. He slipped away.

A few moments later he returned, a basket of food under one arm and a mattress under the other. He set the basket in front of her and then he spread the mattress on the floor. It was his own food and bed he had placed before her.

She wanted to thank him, but he was so hideous she could barely utter a word. She turned away in horror.

"I see that I frighten you," he said. "Do not look at me, but listen. You can stay up here in the daytime, and at night you can roam anywhere inside the church. But do not set a foot outside, day or night. They will catch you and kill you. And if that happens, I would want to die, too."

She was moved by his words. But when she raised her head to thank him, he was no longer there. Then something hairy and shaggy pressed against her hands and knees. "Djali!" The hunchback had rescued him, too. She threw her arms around the goat and sobbed.

The next morning Esmeralda awoke after a long night of sleep. She hadn't slept that well in a long time. She sat up and stretched and saw Quasimodo was peeping down at her through the window. She clamped her eyes shut, then heard his hoarse voice.

"Don't be afraid. I am your friend," he said.

When she opened them again, he was no longer at the window. She hurried over and peeked through. He was bent over, cowering against the wall.

"Come in," she told him, trying to motion him toward her. But he misunderstood and thought she was telling him to go away.

She rushed out and took hold of his arm. He trembled at her touch, yet his whole face beamed with tenderness as she drew him back inside.

Quasimodo hesitated, then spoke. "I am deaf. If you want to speak to me you must do it with signs and gestures. I will also know what you are saying by the motion of your lips and the look on your face."

"Very well," she replied, smiling. "Now tell me, why did you save me?"

"You have probably forgotten about the awful creature who tried to carry you off one night. And the next day, you took pity and brought him a cup of water while he suffered. That was me. I will never forget your kindness on that day. I will do anything for you. I would even jump off this tower if you asked me to." Then he stood.

Esmeralda didn't want him to go. She made a gesture with her hands, asking him to stay.

"No. No. I must leave for now. But I will still look after you." He took a small metal whistle from his pocket. "Take this. Just blow on it when you need me. I am able to hear the sound." Then he laid the whistle on the floor and left.

Esmeralda soon became comfortable in her new surroundings. All the nightmares of the past were fading away. Even her fear of the priest was vanishing with each day. She spent her time thinking only of Phoebus. He was alive! She had seen him there, watching her.

But who was that woman standing with him? *It must have been his sister,* she told herself. *It had to be. Phoebus loves me. He told me himself. But he thinks I'm the one who drove the dagger through his flesh! I must see him. I must tell him about the priest and show him that he is too precious to me. I would never harm him.*

Esmeralda's only friend was Quasimodo. It seemed as though she was more cut off from the world than he was. He looked in on her from time to time, bringing food and water. But he was always careful to keep his face turned away so she wouldn't have to look at his ugliness.

Because of his loneliness, Quasimodo liked to spend time sitting among the frightful gargoyles that looked out from the cathedral. He felt like he fit in among their beastly shapes. Esmeralda overheard him speaking to them. Leaning his head against one of the cold sculptures he said, "Why weren't I made of stone like thee?"

One morning Quasimodo stood behind Esmeralda as she looked out from the roof, watching the people on the street. Then suddenly she spotted her captain.

"Phoebus! Phoebus! There he is!" She waved her arms wildly to get his attention. "Phoebus, can't you hear me?"

Quasimodo, bending forward, saw who she was waving at. It was a handsome young horseman dressed in the regal uniform of a captain. The man rode through the Place de Grève, bowing to a pretty lady standing on a balcony.

Quasimodo could tell by Esmeralda's gestures that the officer was the one she was signaling. He gently tugged her sleeve.

"Shall I bring him here?" he asked.

She fell to her knees, filled with joy. "Yes! Run! Quickly! Bring him to me and I will love you for it!"

He rushed down the staircase, but when he reached the street, all he found was the horse tied to a gate. He looked back up at Esmeralda, still standing in the same spot on the roof. He shook his head sadly, then leaned against one of the pillars on the porch. He would wait until the captain came out, no matter how long it took.

CHAPTER 15

Three Hearts

Quasimodo waited and waited. People came and went from the great mansion, and every time the door opened, he had hopes that it would be the horseman. He would gaze now and then up to the cathedral roof. Esmeralda had not stirred. She remained there, watching.

Time moved on and it was well into the night when the captain finally came out. At first Quasimodo hadn't recognized him because he was wrapped in a dark cloak. But when he mounted his horse, the bell ringer went running after him. "Captain! Wait!"

"What do you want with me?" the captain barked when he saw the hunchback limping toward him.

Quasimodo grabbed the horse's bridle. "Follow me. There is someone who wants to speak to you."

"Let go of my horse, you hideous scarecrow!"

But Quasimodo held on. "There is a woman waiting for you—a woman who loves you very much."

The captain laughed. "A woman as ugly as you, I bet. Tell her to forget me. I am getting married soon."

Quasimodo couldn't hear or understand him. He thought the captain was asking who the woman was. "It is the gypsy girl. She wishes to see you."

This confused Phoebus. On the day of Esmeralda's execution he'd gone back into Fleur-de-lys's apartment. He had not seen the hunchback rescue her.

"The gypsy!" he exclaimed. A feeling of dread settled over him. "But she is dead. Has she sent you here to haunt me?"

Quasimodo pulled on the horse's bridle. "No! Come quickly. This way."

Phoebus lashed the bell ringer across the arm with a whip.

Quasimodo's eyes flashed with anger. "You are lucky to have someone who loves you." He loosened his grip on the bridle. "Go on!"

Phoebus spurred his horse and shot away into the darkness. Quasimodo returned to Notre Dame. He lit a lamp and trudged up the stairs to the tower. Esmeralda had not stirred from her spot.

"You're alone?" She hung her head and wept.

Quasimodo didn't have the heart to tell her the truth—that the captain refused to see her.

"I never saw him," he lied.

She jerked her head up and glared at him. "You should have waited all night!"

Seeing how displeased she was, he slinked back. "I will try to do a better job next time."

"Then leave!" she shouted, trembling.

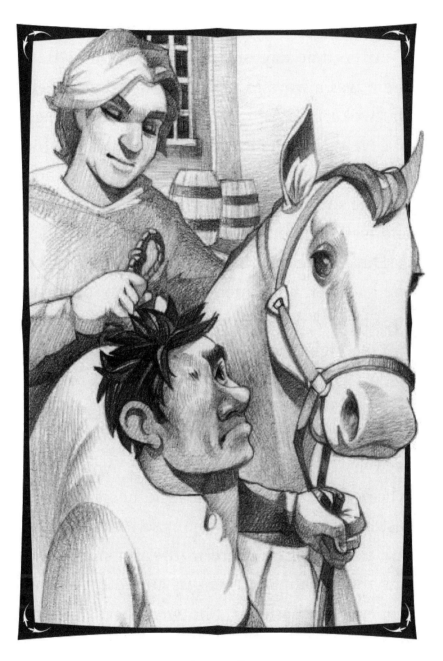

He slipped away, his head drooping.

After that day she never saw him. But, there was always food outside her door when she woke up. And once he'd left her a cage of lovely birds. He liked leaving flowers for her, too. These things should have cheered her, but she still spent her days thinking of Phoebus and watching for him across the square.

Days passed. It had been a long time since she had seen Quasimodo. Was he no longer at the church? Was he hiding from her?"

One night she tossed and turned, unable to sleep. Her mind raced with thoughts of her captain. Where was he? How could she reach him?

"Oh, Phoebus, I must see you," she whispered. Then suddenly, she heard a noise just outside her door. She rose, tiptoed over, and peeked out. There in the moonlight she saw the hunchback. He was curled up on the stones, sound asleep. She went back to bed, happy that he was there to protect her.

Little Sword

Dom Claude Frollo had locked himself away after Esmeralda rejected him. He had barely stirred from his small chamber. But then he found out that the gypsy was alive and hidden within the walls of the cathedral. There were many days when he would sneak up and watch her as she played with her goat.

At night he thrashed back and forth in bed. He could think of nothing but her. She was so close!

One night he came to a breaking point. He could take it no longer. His eyes glared like fire as he leaped from his bed, flung on his black cloak, and rushed out.

Esmeralda was tucked in her room, sleeping lightly. She woke with a strange feeling that someone was watching her. She turned toward the window and a dark, twisted face peered in at her. All the horrors of the past came flooding back.

Then something touched her. She trembled with terror as he grabbed her arms.

"Go away!" she raged.

"No. I won't go. I love you."

She struggled and kicked. "Get out of here, you murderer!" She snatched up the metal whistle and blew. The sound trilled through the room.

Within moments, something grabbed the priest. It was too dark to see, but he was sure it was the hunchback.

"Quasimodo, no!"

Quasimodo drew a sword. He threw the Archdeacon to the floor and pressed his knee against the priest's chest.

Dom Claude tried to signal to the hunchback

that it was his master he'd pinned down, but he was hidden beneath his black cloak. Quasimodo raised the sword high, brought it down toward his head, and stopped.

The hunchback glanced at Esmeralda. "No. I will not let her see me shed blood." He grabbed the priest by his legs and dragged him outside.

Once he was in the light, Quasimodo saw who he'd overpowered and trembled with fear. "Master, I did not know it was you." He handed Dom Claude the sword. "I am sure you wish to kill me now."

But Esmeralda snatched the sword away before the Archdeacon could take it. She held the point of the blade to his nose.

"How dare you come here! You attacked Phoebus and let me believe that he was dead. But I know that he is alive!"

Without a word, the priest dodged away, rushing down the spiral stairs. He locked himself back in his cell, thinking, *If I can't have her, no one shall.*

CHAPTER 17

The Little Shoe

Pierre Gringoire had spent the last few months at the Court of Miracles. He continued performing his balancing act for what little money he could make.

One day as he crossed the square, someone tapped his shoulder. When he spun around, there stood the Archdeacon. Pierre almost didn't recognize him. The man's eyes were sunken and hollow, and his hair had turned the color of snow.

"How are you?" Dom Claude asked.

"So-so," Pierre replied.

The priest nodded. "And how are you earning money these days?"

"With a chair between my teeth," the poet joked.

Dom Claude smiled and Pierre could see the heavy wrinkles creased around the man's mouth. "And what about the gypsy girl?" Dom Claude inquired.

Pierre was stumped by all these questions? "I have not seen her."

"But isn't she your wife? Surely you have tried to speak to her."

"Well, uh, I've been busy," Pierre stammered.

Dom Claude glared into his eyes. "But she saved your life. Now is your chance to save hers. They are still planning to hang her."

Pierre couldn't believe it. "But she has the protection of the church. They can't touch her."

"Yes, they can," Dom Claude said. "Someone has requested a special order from the King."

Pierre stopped to think. "But how can I save her?"

The Archdeacon moved closer and whispered, "You can smuggle her out."

"What? No! They will hang me instead." But then he had an idea. "I know a way. I'll get help from my friends at the Court of Miracles. We will storm the cathedral."

With Pierre's help, King Clopin organized a mob. That night the crowd of thieves and beggars marched to the church, carrying torches, sticks, and an assortment of weapons.

Up in the bell tower, Quasimodo peered over the North Tower and saw them thundering toward Notre Dame. He panicked. Were they here to take Esmeralda? He had to stop them.

When Clopin reached the cathedral door, he shouted, "Bishop of Paris! You have wrongfully accused one of our sisters. Surrender her to us!" And with that, the mob charged the door.

Quasimodo had no way of knowing that they wanted to save Esmeralda. He attacked them, heaving large stones and beams from the roof.

But the army of thieves burst through the door, taking the church on all sides. Quasimodo knew he couldn't fight them off, but he had to protect Esmeralda. He hurried to her room and opened the door . . . but she was no longer there.

When the attack had started, Esmeralda had been sleeping. Then two men had burst in. She was about to scream when, "Esmeralda, wait! It's me, Pierre. Your husband." A mysterious man stood behind him. His cloak and hood covered his face.

"Who is that?" she asked.

"Don't worry," Pierre assured her. "He's a friend. But come with us. You are in danger."

The three of them took Djali and hurried out of the church. They wound through the back streets of Paris until they reached the river.

"There," the stranger said, pointing to a small boat. They all climbed inside and pushed away into the current.

Esmeralda watched the dark stranger. He seemed familiar, but she couldn't be sure. With a gentle bump, the boat reached the opposite shore. The man offered his hand to Esmeralda, but for some reason she couldn't bring herself to touch him. She stepped out of the boat on her own.

She stood for a moment, then turned back toward the water. "Pierre?" But he was gone. He had rowed away, taking Djali with him.

"Now!" the man snapped, grabbing her arm.

"Wait! Who are you? What do you want?" she cried.

He dragged her along until they reached the Place de Grève, where a scaffold and gallows awaited her. It was then that he lowered his hood.

"No!" Her worst nightmare had come true. The wicked Archdeacon stood before her. He leaned in close. She could feel his foul breath on her ear.

"This is where you will hang, my dear. Unless you let me help you. Run away with me. Run away with me now."

She fought to push him off. "Never! I could never be with you. I love Phoebus."

His eyes flashed and his face filled with rage. "Then die!" He latched onto her once again and yanked her across the square.

"Stop! Please!" she begged, trying to keep up with his pace.

He pulled her up to the cell of the old recluse. "Here, old woman!" he shouted, shoving Esmeralda inside. "Here's the gypsy girl. Now you can have your revenge."

Esmeralda stumbled in and fell. Dom Claude sneered. "You have sealed your fate, gypsy girl." He then turned and ran off into the dark night.

The old recluse clasped Esmeralda's wrist and held tight. She was much stronger than she looked.

"I'll call the soldiers now," the woman said. "This time you will hang. I'll see to it."

Esmeralda hung her head, sobbing. "I don't understand. What have I ever done to you?"

"You're a gypsy," the woman answered. "I hate gypsies. You stole my child!"

"But it wasn't me! I've never taken someone's child."

"Then who was it? Have you seen her? Have you seen my little girl?" The old recluse held up the small shoe that she treasured. "This is all I have left of her."

Esmeralda gasped. She opened the little green bag that she wore around her neck. She pulled out a little shoe, identical to the one in the old woman's hand.

The woman trembled. Tears poured down her cheeks. "I don't believe it. You are my daughter!"

Esmeralda threw her arms around her mother and wept. "After all this time I've found you."

But their happy reunion was interrupted by the sound of soldiers' horses.

"I must hide!" Esmeralda cried. "They're coming for me." She crouched in a dark corner.

The soldiers stopped in the square. One of them spoke. "The Archdeacon said she's in there, Captain Phoebus."

She had nothing to fear now. Her Phoebus would save her. "Phoebus!" she called. But her mother place a hand over her mouth. "Shhh!"

A loud crash echoed through the room as a soldier kicked in the door. "Where is she?"

Esmeralda still hovered in the dark. Her mother blocked her from the soldier's view.

"She ran away. Toward the river."

Esmeralda couldn't wait. Her Phoebus was here. She had to see him. She hurried out to where he sat atop his horse. "Phoebus, it's me!"

The captain glared at her as though she were a stranger. He turned to the guard. "Get it over with." And with that, he rode away.

Esmeralda was stunned. The hangman came forward and placed a noose around her neck. "Wait! No!" she begged.

The old woman sprang at the hangman. Like a wild beast, she bit and clawed. He shoved the old recluse so hard her head struck the pavement. In an instant she was dead.

Esmeralda couldn't believe it. There was no one left to save her. With the noose heavy around her neck, the hangman led her up the steps, to the waiting gallows.

The Marriage of Quasimodo

When Quasimodo saw that Esmeralda was gone, he grasped his head in his hands and stamped with rage. He rushed about the church, top and bottom, over and over, in search of her. But she was gone, leaving him all alone.

He cried out in anguish and fell upon her bed. His lovely gypsy girl had been stolen away. Who could've taken her? *Only one person*, Quasimodo reasoned. *The Archdeacon. He had a key.*

Quasimodo descended the staircase to a gallery below. He saw the Archdeacon leaning against a balcony, intently watching some activity. The hunchback followed his gaze.

That's when he saw it—the body of his beautiful gypsy dangling from the end of a rope.

A devilish rage filled him. He rushed the priest, and with his two huge hands, thrust him over the balcony.

Dom Claude grabbed a gutter and held tight. He dared not look at the distant ground below. He tried swinging himself up onto the gutter, but it was too much of an effort. So he hung there, frightened, not sure what to do. The gutter sagged, threatening to break. His fingers began to slip and then the gutter broke, sending Dom Claude plunging to his death.

Quasimodo, torn with grief, still gazed at Esmeralda's lifeless body. Heaving a deep sigh, he cried out, "You are all I have ever loved!"

<hr />

On that day, Quasimodo disappeared. No one in Notre Dame knew where he'd gone. That evening, the hangman and his assistants cut down Esmeralda's body and placed her in a tomb at Montfaucon—one of the most ancient cemeteries in the kingdom.

About a year later, men were sent to Montfaucon to retrieve the body of a prisoner who had been pardoned after death and allowed a decent burial. But once inside, they came upon something quite odd.

There were two skeletons in the tomb, one entwined with the other. One skeleton was a woman wearing a small green bag around her neck. The other was a dwarf with a bumpy, crooked spine. It appeared as though he came there to die.

When the men tried to pull that skeleton apart from the one it held, its crooked old bones buckled and crumbled into dust.